# the bracelet

story by Yoshiko Uchida
illustrated by Joanna Yardley

PAPERSTAR

Penguin Young Readers Group

The author and publisher gratefully acknowledge the help of Donald Daborn in making this book possible. The illustrator gratefully acknowledges the Uno family of Northampton, Massachusetts, for opening their home and library to her, and the Amherst, Massachusetts, Japanese Language School for helping her find the perfect model.

Library of Congress Cataloging-in-Publication Data    Uchida, Yoshiko.    The bracelet / story by Yoshiko Uchida; illustrated by Joanna Yardley.    p.    cm. Summary: Emi, a Japanese-American in the second grade, is sent with her family to an internment camp during World War II, but the loss of the bracelet her best friend has given her proves that she does not need a physical reminder of that friendship. [1. World War, 1939–1945—United States—Juvenile fiction. [1. Japanese Americans—Evacuation and relocation, 1942–1945—Fiction. 2. World War, 1939–1945—United States—Fiction. 3. Friendship—Fiction.]    I. Yardley, Joanna, ill.    II. Title. PZ7.U25Br 1993 [E]—dc20    92-26196 CIP  AC      ISBN 978-0-698-11390-9      30

Emi didn't want her big sister to see her cry. She wiped the tears away quickly, but couldn't wipe away the sadness inside.

"It's almost time to go," her mother called.

And Emi knew they would have to leave their home soon.

She looked around her room. It was as empty now as the rest of the house. Like a gift box with no gift inside—filled with a lot of nothing.

Emi closed her eyes and tried to remember how it had looked. Flowered chintz curtains at the window, her clothes scattered everywhere, her favorite rag doll and teddy bear sitting on the chest.

She could even remember how the whole house looked if she closed her eyes and kept pictures of it inside her head.

Emi and her family weren't moving because they wanted to. The government was sending them to a prison camp because they were Japanese-Americans. And America was at war with Japan.

They hadn't done anything wrong. They were being treated like the enemy just because they *looked* like the enemy. The FBI had sent Papa to a prisoner-of-war camp in Montana just because he worked for a Japanese company.

It was crazy, Emi thought. They loved America, but America didn't love them back. And it didn't want to trust them.

Emi ran to the door when she heard the doorbell. Maybe, she thought, a messenger from the government would be standing there, tall and proper and buttoned into a uniform. Maybe he would tell them it was all a mistake, that they didn't have to go to camp after all.

But when Emi opened the door, it wasn't a messenger at all. It was her best friend, Laurie Madison, who was in the second grade with her.

She hadn't come to walk to school with Emi. And she hadn't come to ask her to go roller-skating. She hadn't come to show her a new dress or to ask her to go to the store with her, either.

She came with a gift, as though she'd come for a birthday party. But she wasn't wearing her good party dress, and she looked just as sad as Emi felt.

''Here,'' she said, thrusting her gift at Emi. ''It's a bracelet. It's for you to take to camp.''

Laurie helped Emi put on the bracelet. It was a thin gold chain with a heart dangling on it, and Emi loved it the minute she saw it.

"I'll never, ever take it off," Emi promised. "Not even when I take a shower."

Laurie gave Emi a hug. "Well, good-bye, then," she said. "Come back soon."

"I will," Emi answered. But she really didn't know if she'd ever come back to Berkeley. Maybe she would never see Laurie again.

She watched as Laurie walked down the block, turning and waving and walking backwards until she got to the corner.

Emi couldn't bear to watch anymore, and she slammed the door shut.

When the doorbell rang again, it was their neighbor, Mrs. Simpson. She'd come to take them to the center where all the Japanese-Americans were to report.

"Come on, Emi. Get your things," her sister, Reiko, called. "It's time to go."

Emi made sure her gold bracelet was secure on her wrist. Then she put on both her sweater and her coat so she wouldn't have to carry them. They could take only what they could carry, and her two suitcases were already full. Each family had a number now, and Emi put tags with their number, 13453, on her two suitcases.

Mama took a last look around the house, going from room to room. Emi followed her, trying to remember how each one had looked when they were filled with furniture and rugs and pictures and books.

They went out for a last look at the garden Papa loved. If he were here now, Emi knew he would pick one of the prettiest carnations and bring it inside. ''This is for you, Mama,'' he would say, and Mama would smile and put it in her best crystal vase.

But now the garden looked shabby and bare. Papa was gone and Mama was too busy to care for it. It looked the way Emi felt—lonely and abandoned.

When they got to the center, Emi saw hundreds of Japanese-Americans everywhere. Grandmas and grandpas and mothers and fathers and children and babies. Everyone was clutching bundles and suitcases tagged with family numbers. Some people were crying, but most just sat quietly. Emi's stomach was jumping up and down, and she wondered if everybody was as scared as she was. She touched the small gold heart on her bracelet and tried to feel brave.

When she saw soldiers carrying guns with bayonets standing at every doorway, she was so scared her knees began to wobble.

"Will they shoot if anybody tries to run away?" she asked her sister.

But Reiko just shrugged. "I don't know," she said solemnly. "Maybe."

Soon it was time for everyone to board the buses lined up at the curb. They would take them to Tanforan Racetracks, which the Army had turned into a prison camp.

As the bus started down the streets she knew so well, Emi kept her eyes on the window. They passed the Kato Grocery Store, where Mama used to

buy bean curd cakes and pickled radishes. The windows were boarded up now, but Emi saw a sign still hanging on the door. It said, WE ARE LOYAL AMERICANS.

I am, too, Emi thought. We all are. But the Army didn't seem to think so.

The bus sped down to the water's edge and crossed the Bay Bridge, looking silvery in the sun.

"Good-bye, bridge," Emi whispered. "Good-bye, San Francisco Bay. Good-bye, sea gulls."

Emi glanced at her sister sitting next to her and could tell she was trying hard not to cry.

"Stupid Army!" Reiko was muttering. "Stupid war!"

And then they were at the Tanforan Racetracks. There was a barbed wire fence all around it and guard towers at each corner. Armed guards swung open the gates to let the buses in and then closed them so no one could get out. They were locked in.

They were assigned to Barrack 16, Apartment #40, and Papa's friend Mr. Noma helped them look for it.

It wasn't among the mass of army barracks built around the racetrack or in the infield. In fact it wasn't a barrack at all. It was a long stable where the horses had lived, and each stall had a number on it.

"Well, here it is," Mr. Noma said as he came to a stall marked #40. "This is your apartment."

Emi and Reiko peered inside. "Gosh, Mama, it's filthy!"

No matter what anybody called it, it was just a dark, dirty horse stall that still smelled of horses. And the linoleum laid over the dirt was littered with wood shavings, nails, dust, and dead bugs. There was nothing in the stall except three folded army cots lying on the floor.

Mama tried to cheer them up. "I'll have Mrs. Simpson send us material for curtains," she said. "It will look better when we fix it up." But Emi could tell Mama felt just as bad as she did. And no one could think of anything more to say.

Mr. Noma went to get mattresses for them. "I'd better hurry before they're all gone," he said. He rushed off because he didn't want to see Emi's mother cry.

But she didn't cry. She just went out to borrow a broom and swept out the dust and dirt and bugs.

It was just after Emi and Reiko had set up the army cots that she noticed.

''My bracelet's gone!'' Emi screamed. ''I've lost my bracelet!''

Emi looked in every corner of their stall and along the ramp that led to their stable. Mama and Reiko helped her, but no one could find it.

It was getting dark, but Mama got out her flashlight and they walked back along the racetrack, retracing every step they'd taken. The track was muddy and full of puddles the rain had left the day before. They looked and looked, but they couldn't find Emi's bracelet anywhere.

It was time now to have supper at the grandstand. Emi stood with Mama and Reiko at the end of a long, weaving line, each of them clutching a plate and fork. But all she could think of was her bracelet. Already she'd lost the one thing that would help her remember her best friend. Emi wanted to cry.

The next day as Emi unpacked her suitcase she found her favorite red sweater. She remembered how she and Laurie had both worn their red sweaters on the first day of school. They'd had matching lunch boxes, too.

And after school they'd gone to fly kites in the vacant lot near home. Emi could just see their red and yellow kites dancing in the wind.

And suddenly Emi knew she was remembering Laurie that very minute, right inside her head. Just the way she could remember every room in her house in Berkeley. Maybe, she thought, she didn't really need the bracelet to remember Laurie, after all.

Mr. Noma came to put up some shelves for them. He'd even made them a table and bench from scrap lumber.

The first thing Mama put on the shelf was a photo of Papa. But Emi knew she didn't need a photo of Papa to remember him.

It was as though Mama had the same thought. "You know, Emi," she said. "You don't need a bracelet to remember Laurie any more than we need a photo to remember Papa or our home or all the friends and things we loved and left behind. Those are things we carry in our hearts and take with us no matter where we are sent."

Emi knew Mama was right. They would soon be sent to a camp in the Utah desert, but Laurie would still be in her heart even there. Laurie would always be her friend, no matter where she was sent. And Emi knew she would never forget Laurie, ever.

## AFTERWORD

In 1942, shortly after the outbreak of war with Japan, the United States government uprooted and imprisoned 120,000 West Coast Japanese-Americans, two-thirds of whom were American citizens.

They had done nothing wrong nor broken any laws, but without trial or hearing they were imprisoned first in abandoned racetracks and fairgrounds, and then sent to ten bleak internment camps located in remote areas of the country.

In 1976 President Gerald R. Ford stated, "Not only was that evacuation wrong, but Japanese-Americans were and are loyal Americans."

In 1982 a commission established by President Jimmy Carter and the United States Congress concluded after an exhaustive inquiry that a grave injustice had been done to Japanese-Americans, and that the causes of the uprooting were race prejudice, war hysteria, and a failure of political leadership.

Six years later the United States government officially acknowledged the injustice of the internment, apologized, and made symbolic restitution to those Americans of Japanese ancestry whose civil rights had been abrogated.

*—Y.U.*